presents the story of
Harvey
Rue and Willy in...

For William

By the same author
THE FOXWOOD TREASURE
ROBBERY AT FOXWOOD
THE FOXWOOD KIDNAP

First U.S. edition 1986
by Barron's Educational Series, Inc.

First published in 1986 by
André Deutsch Limited
105 Great Russell Street, London WC1

All inquiries should be addressed to:
Barron's Educational Series, Inc.
113 Crossways Park Drive
Woodbury, New York 11797

International Standard Book No. 0–8120–5770–8

Library of Congress Catalog No. 86-13988

Printed and bound by L.E.G.O., Vicenza, Italy
6789   987654321

The Foxwood Regatta

Written and Illustrated by
Cynthia & Brian Paterson

BARRON'S

Woodbury, New York

As Willy Hedgehog rushed up the path from the river, he caught sight of his friends Harvey Mouse and Rue Rabbit.

"Wait for me," he shouted. "Something awful's happened. I've just seen the rats ram the squirrels. They're in a fast new boat and they're bound to win."

The Foxwood Regatta was only two weeks away. As usual, Harvey, Rue, and Willy would be in the last race, which the rats, who were good at cheating and bullying, always won. The only rule was that your boat, which could be any kind, must be homemade.

"Let them win," said Rue. "I don't think I'll bother this year."

"I agree," said Willy. "I can't swim and I hate water."

"Stop talking like that," shouted Harvey. "I'm not giving in to those sneaky rats. If you can't beat 'em, join 'em, I say."

Willy looked startled. "What do you mean?" he squeaked. "Ask for a ride in their boat?"

"No, you idiot," explained Harvey. "I mean use cunning. Find out what their plan is and make sure it doesn't work."

"How do we do that?" asked Rue.

"Spying," said Harvey, "so they can't spring any surprises."

Rue's father said they could use the old barn to build their boat. It was on the river bank and just right for launching. They set to work cleaning and tidying it, and were ready to begin work when an argument started. What kind of boat did they need?

"Something strong," said Harvey, "that will smash the rats' bow if they ram us. Remember what Willy saw yesterday."

"With extra thick planks and iron bolts," added Willy.

"Yes," agreed Rue, "and flat-bottomed like a punt so it won't capsize."

"We'd never get it moving," muttered Harvey. "It's no good being unsinkable if everyone's going faster."

"What about a steamboat?" said Rue suddenly. "Plenty of power in steam."

"Less effort than rowing, too," said Willy.

"We can't build anything like that," said Harvey.

They spent so much time shouting and arguing that by the end of the day they hadn't even begun their real work. When Rue's mother arrived she was greeted by three glum faces.

"What's wrong?" she asked. "Can I help?"

"No," said Rue sadly. "We've got a good idea for a boat we can't build."

"Why not ask Captain Otter?" suggested Mrs. Rabbit. "You remember, he used to run the old paddle-ferry . . ."

"That's it! A paddleboat," interrupted Harvey. "Thanks, Mrs. Rabbit. You've probably just solved our problem."

The next day they borrowed a boat and set off to find Captain Otter. Harvey and Rue rowed, while Willy looked out for rats. Before long he spotted three in a very ordinary-looking boat.

"They couldn't do much harm in that, Willy," said Rue. "Are you sure they were capsizing boats yesterday?"

"Yes," said Willy thoughtfully, "but they were in a different boat and there were more of them."

"They've disappeared in the reeds over there," said Harvey. "There must be a hidden inlet. Let's go ashore, then we can creep up and sneak a look at what they're doing."

Peering through the undergrowth they spied the rats fitting sharp, pointed poles into brackets fastened to the sides of a boat.

"Very clever," said Harvey. "Those poles could easily make a hole in a light boat, and they're carried underwater so no one sees them."

"We were right about needing thick planks, then," said Rue, "and about needing speed."

"That's where Captain Otter can help," said Harvey. "Let's go!"

An hour later Willy, in the bow, called out, "Pull over to the bank.
There's something ahead that looks like a houseboat."
It was a houseboat, and, as they drew alongside, they were greeted
by a cheery shout!

"It's Rue, isn't it, with some friends?" asked Captain Otter.
"How's your mother, and what brings you here?"

"We need your help, sir," said Rue. "We're in for the last race in
the Regatta, but we don't stand a chance if we can't outwit the
rats."

"Count me in," said the Captain. "I can't stand those rascally rats, but I'm too old to take them on myself."

He invited them aboard, and Rue told Captain Otter about their plan to build a paddleboat.

The Captain whistled. "It won't be easy, you know," he said.

"We'll do the work," promised Harvey, "if you'll draw the plans."

"Done," said the Captain. "Now you go along home and I'll get to work. We'll meet again tomorrow."

As soon as Rue and his friends had gone, Captain Otter began work. It was no easy matter. Several times he had to tear up the plans and start again, but by midnight the drawings were finished, and by dawn he had built a model. After an hour or two's sleep he set out for Foxwood.

Harvey, Rue, and Willy couldn't wait to get started when they saw the model.

"If our boat is half as beautiful we'll be the pride of the Regatta," said Willy.

Captain Otter beamed. "We'll make the hull first," he said, "then fit the stove, the boiler, and the paddles."

The three friends set to work. First they chose and shaped the planks for the hull, then Willy began nailing them together. Too eager, he hammered a nail so hard it went right through the wood, making a huge hole.

"Clumsy idiot," yelled Harvey. "If you keep bashing like that we'll end up with a sieve, not a boat."

Willy threw down the hammer in disgust. "Do it yourself, if you're so clever," he muttered, stalking off.

"You shouldn't have said that," interrupted Captain Otter. "You know how touchy Willy can be."

"Well, we can't wait all day for him to get over his sulks," sighed Rue, grabbing the hammer. "I'll finish it. He'll feel better in the morning."

Willy did feel better, and he made a good job of tarring the joints. Harvey and Rue screwed down the canopy poles, and Captain Otter helped them fit the rudder and stack the firewood.

"Painting next," he said. "You can do that, Willy."

"Right," said Willy, beginning with a blue stripe. "Now green," he muttered, "and then red, I think."

He stepped back to admire his work and gasped! The colors had all run.

"Ah, well," he said bravely as he wiped off the paint, "that's another mistake I won't make again."

Rue's father arrived with a handsome wooden figurehead, and
Captain Otter fixed a shiny brass funnel. When Harvey's mother
brought a striped canopy their glorious ship was ready.

Harvey, Rue, and Willy were up early next morning to help Captain Otter with the launching. Word had got about and there was quite a crowd on the bank, waiting to cheer the ship on its way.

First the Captain and Rue's father made a slipway, then everyone heaved and pushed. Slowly at first, then with a rush and a splash the paddleboat was floating proudly on the river.

Harvey, Rue, and Willy climbed on board.

"Captain Otter," called Harvey, "we couldn't have built her without you. Will you name her, please?"

"That I will," answered the Captain, smiling happily. He turned to Harvey's mother.

"Have you got it?" he asked mysteriously.

"Here you are, Captain," she said, and handed him a bottle of Squire Fox's special lemonade. The captain broke the bottle on the bow.

"I name this ship *"Duchess of Foxwood,"* he said, and everyone cheered. The three friends were very proud.

As Captain Otter joined Harvey, Rue, and Willy for their first lesson in handling her, the rats rowed slowly alongside.

"Mind you don't run out of fuel before the race," one of them jeered.

Harvey thought of their wood stacks. "No fear of that," he called. "You won't catch us running out of steam."

After supper Harvey, Rue, and Willy settled on board the *Duchess* for the night. After a while Willy awoke with a start.

"Did you hear that?" he asked.

"No, I didn't," said Harvey sleepily. "You must have been dreaming, Willy."

"I was dreaming about logs," Willy replied. "I do hope we have enough."

The first thing Rue heard in the morning was his mother calling them for breakfast.

Harvey peered through the porthole. "Where's Willy?" he said. "His bunk's empty."

"Probably eating breakfast," said Rue.

But he wasn't. Rue's mother said she had seen him setting off along the river bank earlier.

Just as they were starting breakfast Willy strolled in.

"Where have you been?" asked Harvey.

"Just checking the route," said Willy, holding out his plate for a large helping of Mrs. Rabbit's scrambled eggs.

"We've got all day free," said Rue.

"Let's go to the fairground," suggested Harvey.

"And buy some buns," said Willy, who was always hungry.

The scene was set for a
wonderful day. There were
flower sellers, tents, stalls,
picnics, and boating. Mr. Mouse
and Mr. Rabbit tried a bit of
punting, while Mr. Hedgehog
helped the ladies set out the picnic.
Willy and Harvey enjoyed a cup of tea while keeping
a close eye on Rue, who was messing about on the river.

Even Mr. Gruffey, the badger, was there coaching one of the crews, but, unfortunately, his bike got a flat tire.

With only a short time to go before their race, Willy sneaked off to buy more buns, and by the time the Squire of Foxwood arrived at the start a large crowd had gathered.

"My stomach feels funny," said Willy.

"Too many buns," said Harvey unsympathetically.

"No," said Willy, "not buns, rats! There they are now, looking really fierce."

"Well they . . ." began Harvey, but he was interrupted by the Squire calling the animals to get ready for the start of the last race. Harvey, Rue, and Willy hurried to untie the *Duchess* from her mooring and get her to the starting line.

"Ready, get set, go!" called the Squire, and, with a cheer from the crowd, they were off.

The rats dug in their oars and spurted off, narrowly missing a crew of squirrels and sending their sailing dinghy so badly off course it collided with some nervous hedgehogs. A boatload of over-eager mice lost an oar but, surprisingly, the rabbits, paddling a sturdy canoe, had overtaken the rats by the time the *Duchess* had got up steam.

By the time they reached open country the boats were neck and neck. This was the rats' chance. Steering straight for the hedgehogs, they upended their boat against the bank. The poor hedgehogs could only scramble ashore and watch the others go by.

"Did you see that?" shouted Willy indignantly. "Cheats!" And he hurled a sticky bun at the rat captain. Immediately a flour bomb hurtled through the air and burst on his head.

"Full steam ahead," ordered Harvey. "They're coming after us." But as he spoke the *Duchess's* engine spluttered and stopped.

"No logs left," called Rue. "The rats must . . ."

"Crash!"

"They've rammed us," said Willy. "And look — their pole's broken. Hooray!"

Rushing to the side, Harvey and Rue looked over. The rats were all shouting at once, dismayed that their secret weapon had failed.

"Head for the bank," said Willy.

"No," said Rue, "we can't give up now."

"We're not going to," said Willy, "just refuel. I stacked logs along the route this morning — just in case . . . I told you I heard something last night. The rats must have been stealing our firewood."

"Willy, you're a genius," said Harvey.

Once they had fresh logs aboard it didn't take long for the *Duchess* to catch up with the two leading boats. The rats and rabbits were level with each other with only one more bend before the finish.

"More wood," said Harvey, as Willy and Rue threw logs into the stove, "we can still do it." And the faithful *Duchess* fairly flew through the water.

Furious at having victory snatched from them by a boat they couldn't sink, the rats turned on the rabbits.

They bombarded them with flour bombs, and then, when the rabbits could hardly see what they were doing, they drove their oars into the water and shot straight at their boat. There was a tremendous crash, the boat sank, and the rabbits were left splashing about in the water. With a triumphant shout the rats shot ahead.

"Look!" yelled Willy. "They can't swim."

Harvey swung the *Duchess* over to the rabbits. Rue threw out ropes, and they all leaned over to pull the rabbits to safety.

But it was too late to catch up. The rats would win. There would be no first prize for the *Duchess* in spite of her crew's efforts.

"Poor Captain Otter," said Harvey sadly. "He did so want us to win."

"No one's cheering the rats," said Rue suddenly. "Do you think the crowd saw what happened?"

"They might have," answered Willy. "Look, there's the finishing post; we're nearer than the rats realized."

As the rats crossed the finishing line, everyone fell silent. Then, as they grabbed the first prize, they were chased off to boos and hisses and cries of "Cheats" from the crowd.

"Well, we'll be second, anyway," said Harvey. "That's better than nothing." And, with a cheerful toot-toot, they steered the *Duchess* to the finish.

The crowd cheered as Harvey, Rue, and Willy were presented with second prize and first prize for the prettiest boat on the river.

"Well done," said Captain Otter. "I saw what happened, and you're the real winners, in my opinion. I don't think the rats will *dare* to enter next year!"

"I hope they will," said Harvey. "We can beat them if you help."

"Count on me," said the Captain. "Now, let's celebrate. Sticky buns and lemonade all around!"